Rainbow Fish & Friends

Lost at Sea

TEXT BY GAIL DONOVAN

ILLUSTRATIONS BY DAVID AUSTIN CLAR STUDIO

Night Sky Books
New York • London

Rainbow Fish and his friends couldn't keep still. They swished and swirled about the school cave. Today was the big field trip to the Crystal Caverns. They were going to swim to the caves, they were going to see Old Nemo, and they were going to miss school!

"Attention, please," said Miss Cuttle. "The Crystal Caverns are one of our local treasures, but they are not a playground. Our job is to learn all we can and then come back safely to school. Everyone has a partner—younger students will have older buddies."

She called out the pairs: Little Blue and Spike, Rusty and Rosie, Pearl and Dyna, Angel and Puffer, Tug and Rainbow Fish.

Led by Old Nemo, the school fish drifted through the Crystal Caverns.

"Look at me!" said Rainbow Fish. "I match."

Trying to stick close to his buddy, Tug bumped against
the rock crystal. It moved. It was loose!

"Take it," whispered Spike to Rainbow Fish, "Dare you!"

"Double dare you!" Little Blue added.

"I'd give anything for one," Rainbow Fish admitted,
"but I don't know. . . ."
   "Diamonds!" thundered Old Nemo. "Follow me and
we'll see what is called a diamond in the rough!"

Rainbow Fish couldn't wait to see a diamond crystal. He darted off after Old Nemo. Spike and Little Blue followed him and everyone else tagged along.

Everyone except Tug.

Rainbow Fish has been such a good friend, I could get a crystal for him, thought Tug.

But there were so many to choose from, how could he find just the right one? Some were pretty but too bulky to carry or stuck fast to the cavern walls. Others were small, but not beautiful enough for Rainbow Fish. If he just looked a little bit longer . . .

"Let's tell Old Nemo what we learned," said Miss Cuttle at the end of the trip. "Who remembers what the word *crystal* means?"

Dyna piped up, "Clear as ice!"

"I saw crystals as big as icebergs!" bragged Puffer.

Angel said, "The precious gems were simply gorgeous."

Everyone had something to say—everyone except Tug.
"Tug," said Miss Cuttle, "what did you like best? Tug? Tug!"

"Big buddies," cried Miss Cuttle, "find your little buddies!"

When everyone had paired off, Rainbow Fish was all alone. Nobody could remember the last time they had seen Tug.

"We'll never find him," worried Rusty. "I just knew something like this would happen!"

Old Nemo led the search party. "Stay in line!" he boomed. "I don't want to lose any more of you minnows!"

They stopped to call Tug's name, and Rainbow Fish shouted louder than anyone, "Tug!"

The deep caverns only swallowed up his voice. No answer. Rainbow Fish's stomach felt heavy and sick—like he had swallowed a rock crystal. He forced himself to try one more time.

"TUG!" he screamed.

"Over here!" came the answering cry. Old Nemo sped toward the little voice.

"Your attention, please," Miss Cuttle told the reunited school fish. "I may have eight tentacles, but I have only two eyes. We were very worried about you, Tug. You gave us quite a scare."

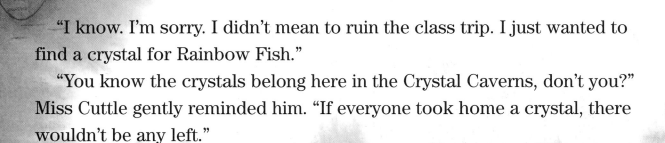

"I know. I'm sorry. I didn't mean to ruin the class trip. I just wanted to find a crystal for Rainbow Fish."

"You know the crystals belong here in the Crystal Caverns, don't you?" Miss Cuttle gently reminded him. "If everyone took home a crystal, there wouldn't be any left."

"I didn't think of that," Tug admitted.

"I'm sorry, too," added Rainbow Fish. "Tug may have been the one who got lost, but I was the one who lost him. I wasn't much of a buddy."

"All's well that ends well," said Old Nemo. "The Crystal Caverns are closing for the day, so off you go. Go on, shoo! But remember to stay with your buddy!"

"We will!" they called, swimming back to school.
"We definitely will!" said Tug and Rainbow Fish.

Night Sky Books
A division of North-South Books Inc.

First published in the United States, Great Britain,
Canada, Australia, and New Zealand in 2001 by
NIGHT SKY BOOKS, a division of North-South Books Inc.

ISBN 1-59014-020-6
1 3 5 7 9 10 8 6 4 2
Printed in Belgium

For more information about our books and the authors and artists
who create them, visit our web site: **www.northsouth.com**